ARABELLA
THE SMALLEST GIRL IN THE WORLD

By Mem Fox

Illustrated by Vicky Kitanov

SCHOLASTIC INC.

New York Toronto London Auckland Sydney

Arabella was the smallest girl in the world.

She had a pillow just like yours,

And a house plant just like mine.

She had a bath that's just like ours,

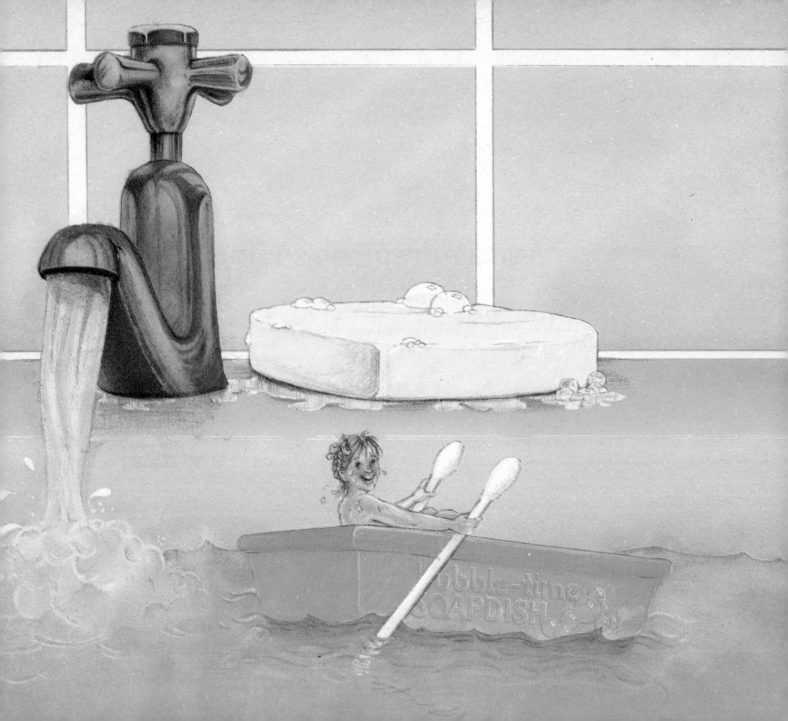

And a mirror, oh so fine!

She had a teddy just like yours,

And a handkerchief just like mine,

She had coat hangers just like ours,

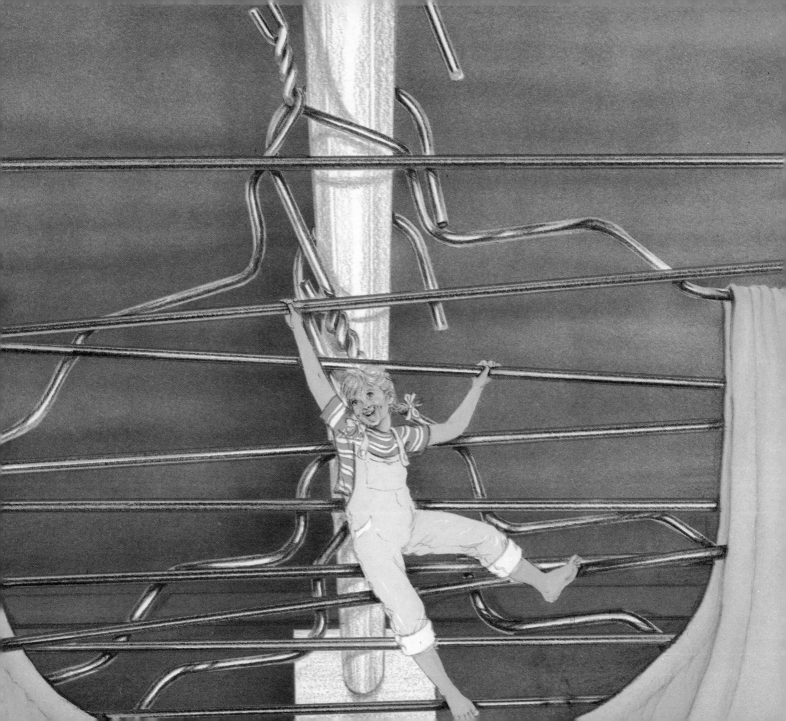

And a dish towel, oh so fine!

She had ice cream just like yours,

And a lamp that's just like mine.

She had pencils just like ours,

And a thimble, oh so fine!

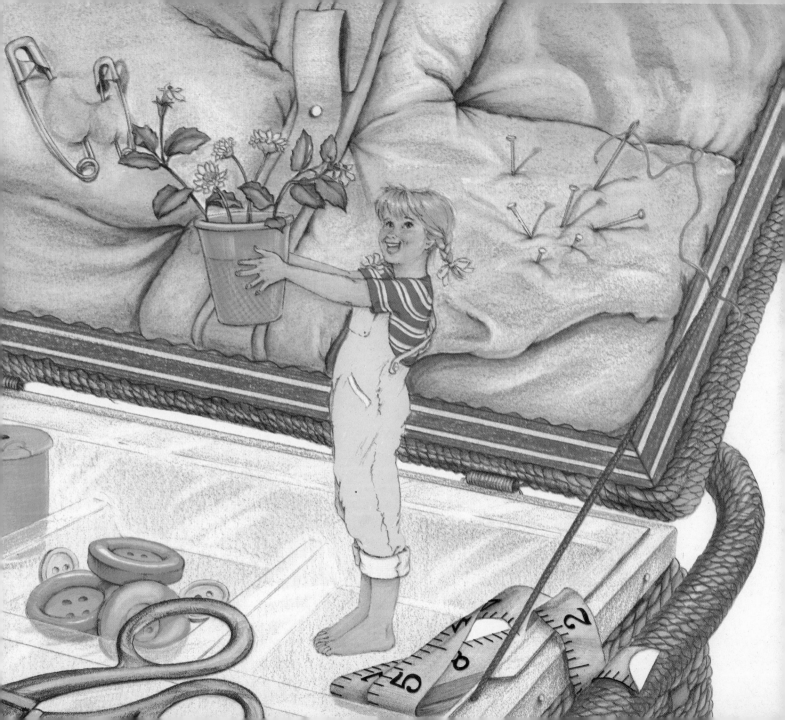

She had a neighbor just like yours,

And a bath sponge just like mine.

She had a story just like ours,

With an ending — oh, so fine!

For Tam

ISBN 0-590-41051-2

12 11 10 9 8 7 6 5 4 3 2 1   7 8 9/8 0 1 2/9

Printed in the U.S.A.   23
First Scholastic Printing, December 1987